HOW T FUN Y

An Extra-Silly Guidebook

by Jovial Bob Stine
inside illustrations by Carol Nicklaus

HA

HA HA HA

HA

HA

HA

HEH

HA

HA

SCHOLASTIC INC.
New York Toronto London Auckland Sydney

ISBN 0-590-44099-3

12 11 10 9 8 7 6 5 4 3 2 1   0 1 2 3 4 5 6/9

Printed in the U.S.A.   40

First Scholastic printing, January 1991

This book is for Jane,
who always knows what's funny.

Contents

Items You Will Need for Following the Lessons in This Book

The following supplies, most of which can be found around the house, are absolutely necessary. Make sure you have them all in front of you before moving on to Chapter One. You will need:

1 200-lb. ball of pink mohair
wax lips (blue)
200 lbs. live bait
   dipped in cheddar cheese
1 four-sided triangle

3 tsp. vanilla
1 radioactive lunch box
1 underwater gorilla feeder
1 mink-lined mink
1 rabbit's-fur squirrel

1 rhinestone weasel whip
three-inch sideburns
  (blue, if possible)
a bronze statue of Lassie
  riding a horse
1 tissue-paper raincoat
  (single-breasted)
1 chicken salami (blue)
1 battery-operated cat
  squeezer

a raisin on a stick
a warm doorknob
gray jelly beans
1 pair goldfish boots
  (high-heeled, if possible)
1 red piano stool
  (without wheels)
1 electric soap dish
1 ferret pie a la mode
a wet llama

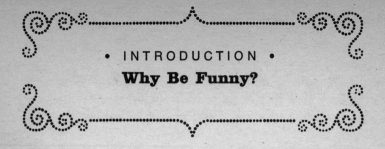

Why Be Funny?

Has this ever happened to you?

You pick up a new book. You just start to read the introduction. And suddenly the book asks, "Has this ever happened to you?"

Well, if this *has* ever happened to you—don't stop reading. It may happen to you again!

Has this ever happened to you?

You know you're not supposed to play baseball in your front yard, but you and some friends decide to risk a small game. Sure enough, you throw the ball a little too hard. You watch as it smashes through the living room window, bounces off your father's head, and lands on the dinner table, cracking one of your mother's best plates.

Now your father is standing over you, holding the lump on his head. "Just give me one good reason," he says, "one good reason why I shouldn't thrash you about the ears and confine you to your room till you're twenty-one!"

Just one good reason. That's all you need.

You struggle. You think. You sweat. Nothing.

You need this book.

And how about you? Yes, you in the orange sweater with the chocolate stains on the sleeve. Has this ever happened to you?

A gang of bullies has been terrorizing kids at your school. Now they've got you surrounded in a deserted corner of the playground. They have an offer to make you—"Your lunch money or your life!"

You've got to think fast. Should you burst out crying? No. Maybe if you can think of something clever to say, if you can make them laugh, they'll think you're cool and let you get away with only minor bruises.

You struggle. You think. You sweat. Nothing. You hand over your lunch money, your belt, your sneakers.

You need this book.

And how about you—the one who's sitting there wondering if there's going to be a third example. Has this ever happened to you?

Your math teacher is yelling at you because you forgot to do your homework for the third night in a row. "Everyone else has learned about the metric system but you," he says angrily. "What should I do with you? What should I do?"

Boy, are you embarrassed! The whole class is staring at you. If only you could think of something funny to say, something to make everyone laugh. Then you wouldn't appear to be such a loser.

You struggle. You think. You sweat. Nothing.

You need this book, too. Admit it!

When you're in a jam, when things get tense, when you have problems—*big* problems—that's the time to crack a joke, walk into a wall, fall on the floor. Does it help? It can't hurt!

You picked up this book just in time. From now on, when disaster strikes, you'll have the last laugh! And, you'll be *getting* big laughs!

Say the baseball you threw crashes through the window, bounces off your father's head, lands on the table, and cracks a dinner plate. Your father says, "Just give me one good reason why I shouldn't thrash you about the ears and confine you to your room till you're twenty-one!"

You turn to him and say, "But, Dad, you always told me to get the ball over the plate!"

Funny!

Say a gang of bullies has you surrounded on the playground and they are demanding, "Your lunch money or your life!"

You turn to them and say, "Do you accept Master Charge?"

Funny!

Say you haven't done your metric system homework for three days, and your math teacher is embarrassing you in front of the whole class by saying, "What should I do with you?"

You turn to him and say, "Take me to your liter!"

Funny?

Well . . . it's a start!

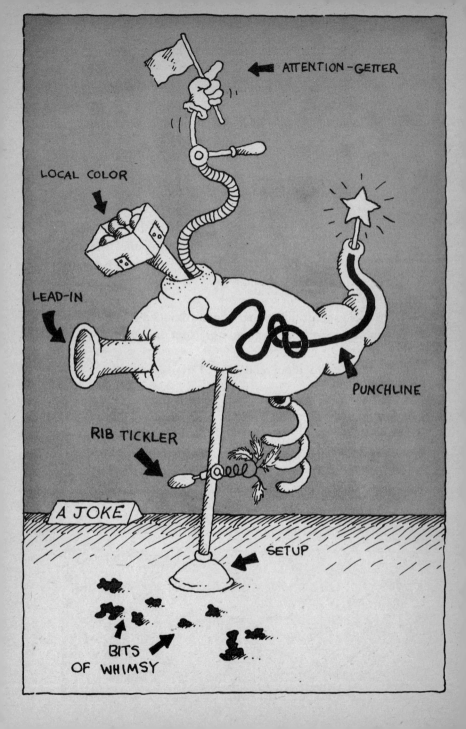

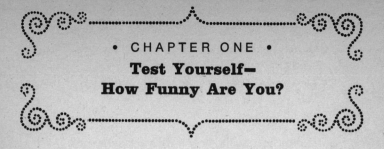

CHAPTER ONE

Test Yourself—
How Funny Are You?

Before we begin our funniness lessons, it's important to find out just how much instruction you need. Perhaps you are already pretty funny and need only to brush up your chimpanzee imitation a bit. Perhaps you are somewhat funny but need to get more wrist action into your jokes. Or maybe you are truly a beginner and should start with something simple, such as falling down a flight of stairs and landing on your head.

This test will show you exactly how much help you desperately need.

PART ONE: RECOGNIZING A JOKE

Here are three items. Only one of them is a joke. Circle the number of the item you believe to be the joke.

1. "Fire! Help! Fire!"
2. "Help! Police! I'm being robbed!"
3. "Boy, am I glad to come in out of the snoo."
   "Snoo? What's snoo?"
   "Nothing. What's snoo with you?"

Here are three different versions of the same joke. Only one version is correct. Circle the number of the joke that is told correctly.

1. "I crossed a carrier pigeon with a woodpecker."
   "What did you get?"
   "I don't know."

2. "I crossed a carrier pigeon with a woodpecker."
   "What did you get?"
   "Nothing. What's snoo with you?"

3. "I crossed a carrier pigeon with a woodpecker."
   "What did you get?"
   "I don't know. But when it delivers a message,
       it knocks on the door!"

PART TWO: PUTTING A JOKE TOGETHER

Here are three jokes. There is something missing in each of them. Guess the missing parts to each joke.

1. "_____
   _____?"
   "I don't know, but it's crawling up your neck!"

2. "_____!"
   "Who's there?"
   "_____!"
   "Irving who?"
   "_____
   _____!"

3. "_____
   _____!"
   "What?"
   "_____
   _____!"
   "Do you mean that—"
   "_____
   _____
   _____!"
   "But I thought you said that—"
   "_____!"
   "Hahaha! That's a riot!"

Here is a joke that's completely scrambled and all out of order. See how long it takes you to put the joke back into its proper order.

"!was it way the just it liked he, No!" .asked
she"?it on anything put you Did" .wife his told
mailman the ",morning this leg my bit dog A"

7

PART THREE:
RECOGNIZING NONSENSE WORDS

To be funny, you must have a large vocabulary of silly words. Here is a list of 10 words. Carefully hidden in this list are 4 nonsense words that aren't real words at all. Can you find the fake words?

homogenized
esoteric
hypothesis
bloopgaloop   *fake*
bleepgaleep
greepgreep
gloopgloop
redundant
sophistry
panacea

8

How good are you at putting these jokes together? The straightlines (serious part) have been separated from the punchlines (funny part). Put the jokes back together by writing the number of the correct punchline next to each straightline. We've done the first one for you.

Straightlines

A. __4__ What has four legs and wears two gloves?

B. ____ What do you get when you cross an ostrich with an ostrich?

C. ____ What's the difference between a raisin and a Red Sox fan?

D. ____ What's black and purple and cries, "Help! Fire! Help!"?

E. ____ What did the kangaroo say to the stuffed pelican?

F. ____ Why did the grape hang around Hollywood and Vine?

G. ____ How many elephants can get into a bad mood?

H. ____ What has five heads and wears four grapes?

I. ____ What's the difference between a grape and a four-legged Red Sox fan?

Punchlines

1. I don't know, but it's crawling up your neck!

2. One has red lips and the other sings tenor!

3. A newspaper.

4. Two baseball shortstops.

5. Nothing. What's snoo with you?

6. When it barks, you'd better listen!

7. Your grandmother in a tree!

8. He wanted to see time fly.

9. The Lone Grape!

SCORING

Give yourself 5 points for every question you were able to answer without slipping off your chair and hitting your head on the wall. Give yourself 10 points for every question you wanted to answer but just couldn't. Give yourself an extra 25 points if you skipped this test and are already halfway through Chapter Two.

0–20 points   You found this book just in time. You are so unfunny, you have to be reminded to laugh when someone tickles you! Perhaps with a lot of hard work you may someday be able to hold your head in the right position to be hit with a pie. But in the meantime, practice crossing your eyes for a while, and we'll get back to you in about 30 pages.

21–50 points   Your idea of being funny is to eat the introduction to this book. Shape up! You'll get indigestion—not laughs—that way. Tying your brother into a slipknot is not funny, either! Untie him and try not to eat the rest of this book.

51–75 points   Not bad, but you still have a lot to learn about being funny. Your idea of a joke is to pour a bowl of raspberry Jell-O down the front of your shirt. Come to think of it, that's *our* idea of a joke, too! Give yourself another 20 points!

76–100 points   Hahahaha! Hohoho Ho ho! Stop! Hahahaha! Please! You're a riot! A riot! Hahahaha! So why aren't you writing your own book?!

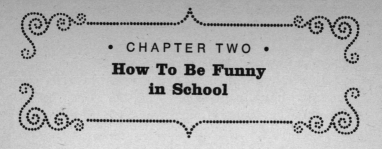

CHAPTER TWO

How To Be Funny in School

If you want to be truly funny, the best place to begin is in school. There everyone sits, hour after hour, five days a week—waiting, waiting for the chance to burst out laughing.

It doesn't take much—a funny noise, a silly mistake, a fall off your seat—and you've got them roaring! Your friends are desperate to laugh—and you'll be ready for them. If you follow the instructions in this chapter, your classmates will begin laughing the moment you enter the room. And they won't stop until you are sent to the principal's office.

ENTERING THE ROOM FUNNY

When should you start being funny? As soon as your alarm clock goes off in the morning, of course! You'll probably want to fall out of bed, put your clothes on inside out, and spill your food all over the breakfast table just to get warmed up.

Then when you get to school, there's one thing you'll

want to keep in mind. You must get the laughs rolling *as early as possible*. You don't want to give your teacher the opportunity to take over the class!

Don't wait for the bell to ring and class to begin. You must start being funny *as you enter the room*. This requires practice, planning, and nerve—but be careful not to overdo it.

Dexter Brewster, who is twelve and should know better, spent six months practicing his Backward Classroom Entrance. Brewster's big plan was to wear his clothes backwards, walk into the classroom backwards, and back into his seat.

We must give Brewster credit for this ambitious attempt, but unfortunately, he carried it out poorly. Instead of backing into his classroom, he miscalculated slightly and backed into the janitor's broom closet. By the time he realized his mistake, he had already been marked absent, the vice principal had phoned his mother to find out where he was, and his mother had phoned the police.

An Important Tip　If you insist on getting laughs by walking backwards, the best place to do it is in the lunchroom. There you can back into people who are carrying trays and cause them to spill their food all over the floor. This is always a big laugh-getter.

Wilma Wallaby, 11, is famous in lunchrooms from coast to coast for what she calls the Double Backward Sur-

prise Bump and Spill. Wilma backs into someone carrying a tray while *she herself* is carrying a tray. Because of Wilma's expert timing, both lunches go flying into the air—and they both land *on the same person's head!* You can imagine the laughs *that* gets.

THE 10-STEP CLASSROOM BUMBLING ENTRANCE

As a special favor to the author of this book, Harrison Babble, 13, winner of 17 awards for classroom disruption, has agreed to set down for you here all 10 steps to his world-famous Clumsy Classroom Clown Entrance. Here is exactly how he performs it, in his own words:

"I wait until they're all in their seats. Then, just as the final bell rings, I step up to the doorway and I (1) bang my head on the door frame, which causes me to (2) drop my books. I (3) bend over to pick up my books and (4) all the change falls out of my shirt pocket. Then (5) leaning down to pick up the change, I (6) rip my pants, (7) stumble over my math book, and (8) break my glasses, causing me to (9) walk into the wall and (10) fall headfirst into the wastebasket."

Of course Babble's 10-step entrance (which he hopes to someday turn into a feature-length movie) will go down in history as one of the great clumsy routines of all time. But as wonderful as it is, many of Babble's classmates wish he wouldn't do it every single morning.

Can you sharpen your pencils for 15 to 20 minutes without stop, keeping a straight face while you grind them down to tiny little stubs despite the attempts of your teacher to conduct class? If so, you should be able to get good laughs at the pencil sharpener.

Timing is what's important here. If your sharpening takes *too little* time, people will think you actually wanted to sharpen your pencils. If your sharpening goes on for too long, people may become annoyed and break your pencils in two.

You must practice when to sharpen and when to pause. Sharpen while your teacher tries to speak, pause when she pauses, and then start sharpening again when she tries again to speak. It may take you a while to get your timing perfect—so bring plenty of pencils!

But don't resort to cheap tricks or props. The unfortunate Dexter Brewster forgot this lesson. Before a recent spelling test, he raised his hand and asked, "Please, Miss Bimmins, may I sharpen my pencil? I only have one."

When Miss Bimmins agreed, Brewster pulled out a specially made pencil that was 8 feet long and weighed more than 50 pounds. The class thought this was pretty funny. But when Brewster tried to lift the giant pencil, he got splinters in his hands and was sent crying to the nurse's office. (The pencil was later chopped up by the school janitor and used for firewood.)

Electric or manual pencil sharpeners—which should you use? Of course there are good arguments for both types. But while the electric sharpener *is* noisier, it doesn't give the good slow, irritating, grinding roar you need to drown out all class discussion and get really big laughs.

Special Warnings   Attempting to sharpen a ball-point pen or felt marker will never get a laugh—unless the ink spurts out all over your clothes. Attempting to sharpen your finger will get you only pity and strange looks.

PASSING OUT PAPERS

Every once in a while a student is given a golden opportunity to be funny when the teacher hands him or her a stack of papers and says, "Please pass these out to the class."

How you manage to mangle these papers, how you scatter them all over the floor, how you tear them, trip over them, spill things on them, how you make sure that no one gets the right paper—that is all up to you.

But just don't pass up this wonderful opportunity to be funny. You may never get a second chance.

MAKING FUNNY NOISES

"Arf arf!"

"Bow wow!"

Yes, the thought of someone barking like a dog in class has you laughing already!

Funny noises are a sure way to get big laughs in school. A loud bubble-gum pop, a hiccup that can be heard down the hall, 20 minutes of uninterrupted coughing—these are all popular and effective. But to be really funny, you must invent original, annoying sounds of your own.

Marlin Milkstraw, 12, is perhaps the noisiest student in the United States. Marlin can be found every day after school perfecting new funny noises in his garage. He always tries out his new noises at the family dinner table before he brings them to school. That way he knows that when the time comes, when the teacher turns her back and he lets go with his new noise, the class will immediately like the new noise and will laugh uproariously until forced to stop.

Although he doesn't like to be taken away from his noise work, Marlin was kind enough to jot down for you his four most effective classroom noises. He recommends that you practice them for at least six months in your room before trying to perform them in class. They are:

- Reep reep
- Yaaaachoooo yaaaachooooo
- Cluck cluck
- Marf marf marf (accent on the second marf)

Marlin warns that after an outbreak of funny noises, most teachers tend to blame the kid with the reddest face. So if you are the kind of kid who blushes easily, it might be best to stay away from funny noises. Concentrate instead on using your red face to get laughs. For example, you might tell everyone you are doing an impression of a cherry tomato.

The Quick Quack While Marlin Milkstraw has invented many extraordinary sounds, the Quick Quack is credited to the multi-talented Harrison Babble. Babble is able to quack with lightning speed in a perfect duck voice. If Miss Pitts turns her back for even a split second, Babble is able to get out a quick "quack," and sometimes an even quicker "quack quack!" Even though Miss Pitts would love to find the quacking culprit in her classroom, Babble's quack is so quick that he has never been caught.

Dexter Brewster, unfortunately, has not been as successful with his version of the Quick Quack. Brewster's

timing was not bad. He waited for Miss Bimmins to turn her back and begin writing on the chalkboard. Then he let go with a very loud "Quaaaaaaaaaacccck!"

And that was the problem. Brewster's quack was much *too* loud. Immediately afterwards, the classroom was attacked by a ferocious flock of wild ducks who were out looking for excitement. Twelve students were severely pecked, and Brewster had to retire his quack forever.

(He tells me that he is currently trying to learn how to oink in French, Latin, and Portuguese, but is having a hard time of it.)

Warning!
These Lines Will Never Get You Laughs in School!

1. "Miss Bimmins, you forgot to assign the homework!"
2. "May I be excused? I think I have the measles."
3. "Miss Pitts, would you ask Billy to stop whispering? I can't hear the class discussion."

4. "My summer vacation was so exciting I don't think I could write it in just one report. Could I hand it in in three installments?"

5. "May I be excused? I think I have whooping cough."

6. "Do we *have* to skip the questions at the end of the chapter? They're very good for review."

7. "I got a 98 on the test. Hope that doesn't spoil the curve for everyone else."

8. "My parents don't care about my grades. They want me to be a well-rounded person."

9. "May I be excused? I think I have the mumps."

10. "Do you mind if I read a few chapters ahead in the textbook? It's so interesting, I just don't want to stop."

11. "For my book report, I read the dictionary. It doesn't have much of a plot, but the author has a great vocabulary!"

12. "A movie?! But you promised us a quiz today!"

13. "May I be excused? I think I have Gwort's palsy."

14. "Could I stay after school and clean up the room for extra credit?"

QUESTIONS FOR REVIEW

1. Is it funnier to enter the classroom on all fours, carrying your books in your mouth—or walking on your hands, wearing a hat on your feet?

2. List the four funniest replies for when your teacher says, "Good morning, everyone. How are you today?"

3. Describe the three best ways to use the water fountain to squirt people halfway down the hall.

4. What is the funniest thing to say when you find you've got your head caught in your desk?

5. What are the two funniest things you can do with spinach in a crowded lunchroom?

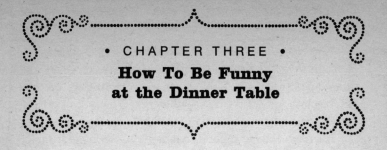

CHAPTER THREE

How To Be Funny at the Dinner Table

It's dinnertime. Perhaps the best time of day to be really funny.

The whole family is together. Everyone is in a good mood. The table is filled with laugh-getting props: dishes to juggle, silverware to toss, food to play with—dozens of opportunities for you to get really big laughs.

The first rule to keep in mind when planning your dinnertime hilarity is this: You must avoid tired old routines that everyone has seen time and time again. Do not even consider such weary old standards as:

1. leaning back in your chair until you fall over.
2. trying to eat Jell-O with your hands.
3. laughing while you drink so that the milk pours out your nose.

These gags will get you only groans—not laughs—and you will probably be deprived of dessert. Save these routines for lunchtime in your school cafeteria where they will be appreciated—especially since everyone at your table will be doing them.

23

If your family uses a tablecloth on the dinner table, you are in luck. The tablecloth can get you more laughs than a box full of wet napkins! If your family does not use a tablecloth, demand that they buy one. You will never get laughs with place mats—no matter how hard you try.

Harrison Babble reports that some of his biggest tablecloth laughs came from simply wiping his mouth on the tablecloth. Babble uses a long sweeping motion for his wiping and generally manages to cover 4 to 5 feet of tablecloth with each wipe. We do not recommend this gag in homes where the laundry is done by hand.

Always keep your tablecloth gags as simple as possible. The unfortunate Dexter Brewster forgot this rule in planning a recent tablecloth joke, with predictable results.

Brewster prepared for his gag one afternoon when his parents were away. Using a hacksaw, he quietly cut a large circle out of the center of his dining room table. He placed a tablecloth over the table to cover the hole. Then he set the table for dinner.

Dexter's delighted parents returned home after a long day of shopping and thanked him again and again for setting the dinner table. Dexter just smiled.

Came dinnertime. Everyone was seated around the table. Dexter decided it was time for his joke. He dropped from his seat and silently crawled underneath the table. Then he quickly stood, popping his head up through the hole in the center of the table beneath the tablecloth, and cried out, "Hi—I'm Casper the friendly ghost!"

The joke was not a success.

The family now has its meals around a card table—a constant reminder to Dexter of just how misguided his poor joke was.

Other Tablecloth Rules

1. It's always funnier to rip a tablecloth with your bare hands than to cut it with scissors.
2. Spilling food on a tablecloth is not funny. Rubbing food into the tablecloth is funny.
3. Wearing a tablecloth around the house is funny. Wearing one to school is not funny.

BEING FUNNY WITH SALT AND PEPPER

To be funny at the dinner table, you've got to start with salt and pepper. Until you have mastered these basic ingredients, you will never be funny with garlic powder and Worcestershire sauce.

Wilma Wallaby kept a collection of salt and pepper shakers handy in her room so that she could practice being funny with them whenever she got a spare moment. Wilma's parents always wondered why she was constantly giggling in her room. They didn't realize how funny salt and pepper shakers can be—if you know how to use them improperly.

Harrison Babble's 3-Step Pepper Sneeze never fails to win him big dinnertime yuks. But other kids report that their parents become alarmed by any kind of sneezing. Instead of getting laughs with their sneezing routines, they find themselves sent to bed with aspirins, extra blankets, and a hot-water bottle. If you wish to risk it, here are the three steps that have made Babble's Pepper Sneeze world famous:

Step One Ask politely for the pepper shaker. Hold it up to your nose and inhale deeply in an extremely exaggerated manner.

26

Step Two   Tilt your head back, open your mouth, close your eyes, and go, "Ah-ah-ah-ah . . ." as if you are about to sneeze. Do not sneeze.

Bring your head back to normal position. Sigh to show that the need to sneeze has passed. Lift your fork as if to eat. Suddenly tilt head back again, open mouth, close eyes, and go, "Ah-ah-ah . . ." Lower head. Do not sneeze. Sigh again. Pick up fork.

You may repeat this as many as seven or eight times.

Step Three   Begin to eat, saying, "There. Thank goodness that's over with." Pause one second. Then sneeze as hard as you can all over the dinner table.

Harrison Babble reveals that he heightens the effect of the sneeze by placing both hands under the table and shaking the table vigorously as he sneezes. Of course his family is horrified and disgusted. After they have stopped laughing, he always says, "Excuse me."

TOO MUCH SALT

Wilma Wallaby gets such big laughs with her Too Much Salt routine, that she doesn't mind spoiling her entire dinner to get them. Wilma's gag is good for dinner table beginners because it requires no preparation and little intelligence. Here's how it works.

Wilma waits until the food has been served. She tastes her meat, frowns, and then says, "Please pass the salt." She shakes some salt onto her meat and returns the salt shaker to the head of the table.

She immediately tastes her meat again, frowns, and says, "Please pass the salt." The salt is passed to her, she sprinkles a great deal more onto her meat, and returns the salt shaker to the head of the table.

Wilma repeats her requests for more salt until her meat looks exactly like Mount McKinley covered with snow. When there is so much salt on her plate that the meat cannot even be seen, she tastes it, smiles, and says, "Great dinner, Mom—but I think the meat is a little too salty!"

According to Wilma, this gag never fails to crack her family up. And she says they laugh even harder as they force her to finish every last bite of meat she has ruined!

TABLETOP TERPSICHORE

Dexter Brewster's Salt Dance is not recommended—even by Dexter himself! Dexter tried the gag only once. He poured about an inch of salt onto the dinner table, jumped up onto the table, and began tap dancing on the salt.

The salt gave a nice, sandy, brush sound to Dexter's dancing, and his family seemed to enjoy the routine for a moment or two—until Dexter kicked the turkey off the table and fell headfirst into the mashed potatoes.

Dexter says that when he can walk again, he plans to give up his dancing career.

Dinner Table Gags To Avoid if at All Possible

1. Sticking a celery stick out of each side of your mouth and saying, "Look, Ma, I'm a walrus!"

2. Buttering your napkin and complaining about how they don't make white bread like they used to.

3. Saying to the person next to you, "What's that slop you're eating?"

4. Holding a watermelon on your stomach and saying, "Do you think this can be surgically removed?"

5. Saying, "Let's not cry over spilt milk," after you've spilled your milk.

6. Placing a fried egg over each eye and asking your parents if they think you need glasses.

7. When tomato soup is served, saying, "Drink your blood before it clots."

8. Placing a banana in your ear and saying, "I can't hear you. I've got a banana in my ear."

9. Whinnying like a horse when hamburgers are served and saying, "Ma, I think this one's still alive!"

10. Holding a canary under your shirt and saying, "Ma, I don't think I can finish my vegetables. Look—my stomach is all fluttery."

11. When your mother serves quiche Lorraine, lobster Newburg, and chocolate mousse, saying, "Aw, Ma, we had this for lunch in the cafeteria today!"

QUESTIONS FOR REVIEW

1. What are the three funniest things you can say with a mouthful of lima beans?

2. True or false—One handful of mashed potatoes can never be as funny as two handfuls of mashed potatoes.

3. What are the best vegetables for throwing? For sitting on? For swimming in?

4. Where are the two funniest places to stick your fork when you are told not to play with your silverware?

Important Advice!

We interrupt the funniness lessons to bring you this important advice from the National Institute of Advice About Anything at All.

What To Do if a Buffalo Becomes Sick on Your Carpet

1. Don't panic.
2. Stay calm.
3. Don't get nervous.
4. Keep cool.
5. Try not to be alarmed.
6. Don't worry yourself excessively.
7. Don't get excited.
8. Try to relax.
9. Don't allow yourself to become agitated.
10. Move to a new town as quickly as possible.

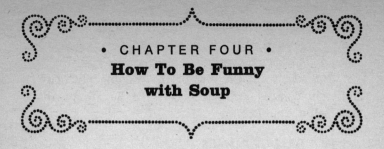

CHAPTER FOUR

How To Be Funny
with Soup

Ahh, soup! Of course, soup must have its own chapter!

Soup is funny as soon as you say it.

Go on—say the word. Soooooooooooooop. It sounds like you're slurping it right off a big spoon. (And, of course, slurping is just one of hundreds of ways to be funny with soup.)

Rule Number One for getting big laughs with soup: Keep it simple.

Dexter Brewster recently learned this lesson the hard way. As part of his elaborate planning, he borrowed a pet rabbit from a friend. When his family was comfortably seated around the dinner table, Dexter carefully deposited the surprised rabbit into his soup. He waited until all eyes were on him, and proclaimed, "Look, Ma, there's a hare in my soup!"

Funny? Perhaps. But Dexter had no time to enjoy his laugh. The rabbit jumped out of the soup (which was mock turtle, actually), scampered through the salad (tossed), raced over the roast beef (medium rare), and began to run in frantic circles about the living room

(French Provincial). The family finally caught the rabbit half an hour later. By that time, the dinner was ruined and the joke had been forgotten.

Brewster spent the rest of the evening practicing a different comedy technique—How To Be Funny All by Yourself in Your Room.

TWO HALL-OF-FAMERS

Now we must take time out to mention two girls who, surprisingly enough, both live on the very same block in Weehawken, New Jersey, and have the exact same name, but do not know each other. Both girls are named Jeri Jean Jerryjene, and both were recently inducted into the Funny with Soup Hall of Fame.

Jeri Jean (the first one—not the other one) is twelve and has won worldwide recognition for her ability to crumble astounding quantities of crackers into her soup. During last spring's Cracker Crumbling Finals (you probably watched them on TV), Jeri Jean broke the world's record by crumbling 3,452.4 saltines into a bowl of cream of tomato. Unfortunately, she also broke the bowl and was disqualified.

When she begins crumbling crackers at the dinner table, Jeri Jean uses both hands at once, sometimes crumbling so hard that she cracks a knuckle. This never fails to get big laughs from the rest of her family, who are also terrific cracker crumblers in their own way.

The other Jeri Jean (who will probably be more surprised than anyone to learn that she is not the only Jeri Jean) has been in the soup spotlight for years because of her ability to eat her soup using strange and totally improper utensils. Jeri Jean began what she calls her Soup Capades at the age of four months by eating her strained vegetable soup with a fork. This always created such hilarity in her house that she began experimenting.

At the age of seven, she began getting big laughs by eating her soup with a sandbox shovel. By the time she was eight, she was skillfully using a dustpan to slurp her chicken noodle. At nine, she had her family in an uproar when she consumed a bowl of minestrone using a specially lined baseball cap.

At present, she is practicing eating her soup with a pair of argyle socks, using a soak-and-suck technique. We expect even bigger things from Jeri Jean in the future.

THE EYES HAVE IT

Harrison Babble (voted Funniest Kid in the U.S. with Soup—until he gave it up to concentrate on being funny with watermelons) has always believed that simple soup gags are the best. Babble used only a Ping-Pong ball and a felt pen for one of his classic soup laugh-getters.

Babble took the felt pen and drew a large, solid brown dot on the Ping-Pong ball. He hid the ball in his shirt pocket, sat down at the dinner table, and waited for the soup to be served.

When no one was looking, he placed the Ping-Pong ball with the large brown dot into his soup. Then he stretched a wide smile across his usually serious face, and loudly proclaimed, "My favorite! Cream of eyeball soup!"

Babble's family was sickened at first. But when they realized that it was not a real eyeball floating in the soup, they laughed for hours.

Babble attempted to follow this triumph a few weeks later by placing *two* Ping-Pong balls in his soup, and saying, "Please tell my soup not to stare at me!" But this time he was firmly told to shut up and eat.

He thus learned Rule Number Two when it comes to being funny with soup:

Don't press your luck.

Other Rules for Being Funny with Soup

1. Placing strange objects in your soup almost always gets a laugh. Attempting to wear your soup is usually less successful.

2. While some kids get big laughs by trying to eat their soup with a fork, other kids attempting this gag are asked to leave the table.

3. Placing your feet in your soup is recommended only if your parents think that *everything* you do is adorable.

4. Any gag that ends with the punchline "But, Ma, you told me to use my noodle!" is probably not worth the effort.

QUESTIONS FOR REVIEW

1. What were the four funniest words ever spelled with alphabet soup?

2. List the three best vampire jokes to tell while eating tomato soup.

3. True or false—It's funnier to spill a soup with noodles than a soup with rice.

4. How many possible ways are there to get a soup spoon caught in your mouth?

Hi, it's me, Dexter Brewster. I suppose you've heard about my funny walk, and you want to learn how to do it. Well, it isn't as easy as it looks. And of course you'll never be able to do it exactly as I do. But I'll try to teach you some of the basic moves.

Watch carefully.

Did you see that? Did you see how I bend my knees just a little? Watch. First this knee, then this knee—but not too much. See—this isn't funny. But this *is* funny.

Now watch my ankles. It takes a while to get them strong enough to bend like this. But you should be almost as good at it as I am in three to four months. Are you watching? See how I dip my shoulders and cross my eyes?

Okay, now for the hard part. First I go up on my toes and then I—whoooops!

Ow.

Oh boy. I sprained it this time. Sprained the ankle. Look. It's swelling up like a sausage.

I think that's the end of your first lesson. You're doing great!

At any party, there is always one person who has the most fun. That person is the one getting all the attention, making all the noise, being funny every second, and keeping everyone else from having a good time. With a little hard work and practice, that lucky person can be *you!*

Of course, there are many ways to disrupt parties and keep everyone laughing until you are asked to leave. In this chapter, we are going to learn the techniques of two experts. Jeremy Jejune, 13, and Gene Willikers, 12, are so successful at being funny at parties, they haven't been invited to any in more than three years!

As funny as Jeremy and Gene are, you can learn from their mistakes. We're going to follow each of them as they try to get big yuks at a party. Follow their moves carefully. And keep a list of the mistakes each of them makes. After we watch them in action, we'll review each performance and take a look at the errors they made.

THE PHONY-SOPHISTICATE APPROACH

Jeremy's biggest accomplishment is the ability to sound totally insincere while being as polite and well mannered as one can possibly be. He affects a slight British accent when he talks, and he's always bowing and kissing hands and saying, "Thank you ever so much" and "Indubitably" and polite things like that—*and he gets big laughs by doing it so well!* Jeremy's manners are so sophisticated, so suave, and so unbearably sickening that people start laughing the moment he tips his hat, bows from the waist, and says, "Beggin' your pardon, ma'am," whenever anyone—male or female—passes by.

Follow carefully now as Jeremy tries out his phony-sophisticate approach at a party. He is coming up the walk now, ringing the bell at the front door to Alice Begonia's house. Alice opens the door. She seems a bit surprised to see him there, his hands behind his back. "Why, hello, Jeremy," she says.

Jeremy bows from the waist and says, "Thank you ever so much for the invitation, my dear young woman. It was so good of you to have me."

Alice looks puzzled. Jeremy steps into her living room, his hands still behind his back. "Oh, what a delightful room!" Jeremy exclaims. "The atmosphere you've created is so celebrational! Allow me to present you with this small token of my esteem, and please accept my heartfelt and fondest regards on this, the anniversary of your birth."

Jeremy reveals that he is carrying a pecan pie in his hands. He presses the pie into Alice's face and looks about the room, eager to accept his laughs.

Did you spot the mistakes Jeremy made? Keep thinking about his performance as you read about Gene.

As much as they try, people just can't hide from Gene at parties. Gene is one of those rare individuals who is willing to do anything he can think of to get laughs at parties. Here he comes now. See if you can spot the mistakes he makes.

Gene walks up to the front door wearing a stuffed parrot on his head. Alice greets him and opens the door. Gene has wax fangs in his mouth. "Fangs a lot for inviting me," he says, spitting the fangs onto the floor.

"Hi, everyone!" Gene walks into the room on his hands so that everyone will notice that he has arrived. "What do you get when you cross a penguin with an elephant?" he shouts. "You get an animal in a very tight-fitting tuxedo! Hahahahaha! Oh, well . . . things are tough all over. Don't applaud—just throw money! Hahahahaha!"

Gene turns to Alice. "Thanks again for inviting me. It's nice to have such a close friend. What did you say your name was?"

Gene pretends to trip on the carpet and flings himself headfirst into the punch bowl. "Delicious," he says, wiping his face off on the tablecloth.

He puts a lamp shade on his head and walks around the room telling everyone, "I feel a little light-headed today!"

When he knows everyone is watching him, Gene walks up to the big chocolate birthday cake and puts his fist through it. "Hey, it's real!" he yells, acting surprised. "Hahaha! How about that!" At this point, Alice's parents ask him to leave.

What mistakes did Gene make? Let's go back and review both performances.

RATING THE PERFORMANCES

Jeremy made several rather serious blunders. Did you catch all these?

1. He was dressed as a turkey, but the party was not a costume party. The hideous green feathers he had pasted all over his body totally ruined the sophisticated effect he was trying to create.

2. It was not a birthday party. It was a Groundhog's Day Eve party. His birthday gift for Alice was not at all appropriate.

3. It was not Alice's party. Susan, who lived three blocks down the street, was giving the party. In fact, Alice wasn't even invited to the party. Therefore she had no idea what Jeremy was doing, bursting into her house dressed as a turkey.

4. Jeremy was a week early. The party was scheduled for the *next* Saturday.

5. The pecan pie was stale.

Gene, on the other hand, made no mistakes.

GIVING YOUR OWN FUNNY PARTY

Harrison Babble, who has received 17 awards for just *staying away* from parties, prefers to give his own parties —at least seven or eight a week. Babble plans his parties so that he is the only one to enjoy them. Recently, he gave one of the funniest parties ever—and Babble himself was the only one laughing! Here's how he did it.

Babble invited thirty kids to this party. He told ten of them that it was a costume party and he insisted that they come in the wildest costumes they could imagine. He told ten others that it was a dress-up party and that they were to come in their best clothes. The remaining ten were told that it was to be a come-as-you-are party, to wear jeans and T-shirts, and the like.

Of course, when everyone arrived, there was great confusion. The kids in jeans and T-shirts felt underdressed; the kids in their best clothes felt overdressed; and the ten who had spent days putting together their costumes felt ridiculous! When he saw them all together, Babble knew his party was going to be a big success.

While they were busily puzzling over each other's attire and arguing over who was dressed correctly, Babble passed out party hats and noisemakers. Before the party, he had carefully cut all the rubberbands on the hats so that no one could keep his hat on for more than a second or two. And Babble had fixed the noisemakers so that they wouldn't make any sound at all—no matter how hard anyone blew into them.

Babble's guests were so busy trying to keep their party hats on and trying to get their noisemakers to work, they didn't notice that Babble had turned the room temperature up to 95 degrees. The phonograph had been carefully stacked with stereo records of wild ostrich cries and train wrecks, so no one was dancing. And the record player was turned up so loud, no one could talk.

"Let's play charades," Babble suggested. Everyone was eager to play—just to be doing something. They quickly divided into two teams. Imagine everyone's surprise when Babble's team drew very easy phrases to perform such as "bird dog" and "catfish"—while the other team found themselves having to pantomime lengthy philosophical tracts, all in Latin!

Since the kids grew tired of charades very quickly, Babble suggested another game, one to be played outdoors. This game involved raking all the leaves in Babble's front yard. (Babble had promised his father that this task would be performed.) The game took several hours, and everyone was greatly relieved when Babble finally announced, "Refreshments are served!"

The party moved to the dining room. Babble brought out three cupcakes and two small bottles of grape juice. "Hope there's enough for everybody!" he said, unable to hide his amusement.

None of the guests would agree with Babble that this was the most successful party he had ever given. But Babble admitted that weeks later, he was still laughing about it.

Perhaps there is a lesson here for all of us.

Perhaps not.

Three Funny Party Games

(Recommended by Harrison Babble)

1. Pin the Tail on Mommy
2. Spin the Birthday Cake
3. Veterinary Surgeon (if you have pets)

QUESTIONS FOR REVIEW

1. True or false—A party needn't end in bloodshed to be truly funny.
2. List the five funniest items that should be "accidentally" spilled on a carpet to liven up a party.
3. Which is funnier—wearing a lamp shade around your waist or stuffing an ice cube down someone's back?
4. Describe the three most popular ways of wearing a birthday cake.

Important!

We interrupt the funniness lessons to bring you this important fish chart from the Important Chart Institute.

Fish Mileage Chart

(All data is from 1955)

Model of fish	Miles per gallon (Fish swim uphill except when swimming downhill.)
Trout	35 in fresh water, 30 in salt water, 0 on highway
Bass	33 in fresh water, 30 in stale water, 0 on highway
Shark	30 in salt water, 30 in lukewarm water (with ice cubes)
Another shark	12 in water, 0 out of water
Swordfish	
(without sword)	11 in blue water, 9 in chocolate milk
(without fish)	0 in gray water, 0 in seltzer water
Tennis sneaker	— (not a fish)
Fish stick	9 baked, 8 broiled, 7 eaten frozen
Guppy	undecided

$416 round trip (weekdays)
(Dry-clean only)

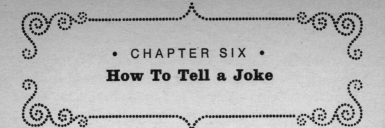

CHAPTER SIX

How To Tell a Joke

"This joke is never going to end!"

"When already? *When* already?"

"I hope I never hear another joke as long as I live!"

Do people say these things when you're telling a joke? If not, you need more practice with your joke-telling.

A truly unforgettable joke should be so long, so confusing, and so unbearably tiresome that the listener *can't wait* to start laughing at the punchline.

Wilma Wallaby is known as the best joke teller in her school, and is widely avoided for that reason. Wilma has been known to stretch a two-line grape joke into a three-day activity, leaving her audience so desperate to get away that they'll laugh at every word she says.

Here is Wilma now, telling one of her shorter jokes. Follow her technique—then practice it yourself on anyone you can force to listen.

Stop me if you've heard this one before. A bear goes into a restaurant. No—it was two bears. That's right. Two bears go into a restaurant, and—wait a minute! No, I got it wrong. It was a giraffe. That's right. A giraffe goes into a restaurant. Only it wasn't really a restaurant. It was a shoe store.

This giraffe asks the clerk for a hot fudge sundae. Oh. I guess it was a restaurant after all. Well, it was more of a diner. There was a counter and a few seats in back. And it was called Joe's Diner. Or was it Jim's Diner? No, I think Jim owned the shoe store. Well, this is the wrong joke anyway.

A bear goes into a diner and orders a hot fudge sundae. He wants to play the jukebox, but there isn't one. "How come you don't have a jukebox?" the bear asks the waiter.

"I don't know," the waiter tells him. "You're the first one to ask me that question."

"Well, that's okay," the bear says. "It isn't part of this joke anyway."

Well, the waiter brings the bear his banana split. Oh, wait—the bear ordered a hot fudge sundae. I guess it was the giraffe that ordered a banana split. That's another joke. Do you know the joke about the giraffe and the banana split? I'll tell that one when I finish this one.

So the waiter says to the—uh oh. I think it was a waitress. That's right, a waitress. She says to the giraffe—er, to the bear, "Are you the one that ordered the snoo?"

And the bear says, "Snoo? What's snoo?"

And the waitress—oh no—that's another joke. Wait. I'll get this right. The waitress brings the bear his hot fudge sundae. Or was it a banana split? No, it was a chocolate sundae with a banana. You haven't heard this joke before, have you? Oh, good.

Well, the waitress goes back to see the boss. Joe. Or Jim. No, Joe. And she says, "What shall I charge him for the pair of knee boots?"

And Joe says, "This is a restaurant—not a shoe store."

And so the waitress says, "What shall I charge him for the sundae?"

And the owner says, "Well, he's only a bear. He probably doesn't know much about what things cost. So charge him five dollars for it."

The bear eats his sundae. Well, almost all of it. I think he left the banana. Of course, I know a great joke about a bear and a banana peel. Remind me to tell it to you when I'm finished. The waitress tells the bear, "That'll be five dollars."

The bear pays the five dollars. I believe he had five 1-dollar-bills. Or was it four dollar-bills and four quarters? Three quarters, two dimes, and a nickel? No, no—I remember! That's right—he had traveler's checks.

Anyway, he pays the five dollars. And as he's walking out, the waitress asks him—

Oh, wait. I think it was a giraffe after all.

No. No. It was a bear. And the waitress asks him, "Why did you choose this restaurant? We don't get many bears in here."

And the bear says, "Nothing. What's snoo with you?"

Oh, no. That isn't right. The waitress says, "Why did you come here? We don't get many bears in here."

And the bear says, "Well, with these prices I can see why!"

Hahahahaha hahahahahaha!! Funny? Hahahahaha!

Joke-Telling Rules

How can you tell jokes as well as Wilma Wallaby? By following these simple rules of joke-telling Wilma was kind enough to write down for you:

1. Always begin by saying, "Stop me if you've heard this one before." If someone says they've heard it, go right on telling it anyway.
2. Gesture a lot with your hands. Stand real close to the person you're telling the joke to, and poke him or her in the ribs to emphasize every third word of your joke.
3. Never tell a joke that takes less than 20 minutes.
4. Never tell a joke that involves a gorilla and a wise old farmer.
5. If you must tell elephant or grape jokes, never tell less than thirty at a time.
6. Always be the first to laugh at your own joke. Laugh as hard as you can so that the others will know just how funny it is.

QUESTIONS FOR REVIEW

1. Was it a bear or a giraffe?

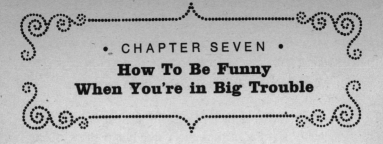

CHAPTER SEVEN

How To Be Funny
When You're in Big Trouble

Now you've done it!

You know you're not supposed to chase the dog through the living room. But you did, and now you've tripped and cracked a mirror, ripped the new upholstery off the couch, pulled down the drapes, knocked the top off the piano, and tipped over the goldfish bowl. You're standing ankle deep in water, clinging to the wet drapes to stay afloat, and you hear your mother approaching, calling, "What's going on in there?"

Now what do you do?

Forget how to speak English? Try to blame the dog for turning the room into a national disaster area? Beg for mercy? Plead insanity? Pretend that nothing has happened?

No, forget all that. You are in BIG trouble—and the only way out is to be funny. Get the injured party laughing, and your troubles are over—at least until they stop laughing!

Dexter Brewster has been in big trouble more often than any other kid in North America (counting Canada

55

and Mexico). During one 24-hour period a few weeks ago, Brewster managed to find himself in these rather unpleasant situations:

- *caught* writing his name in ink on his younger brother.
- *caught* trying to hide his peas in his pants cuffs.
- *caught* signing his parents' name to a petition to ban all homework in school.
- *caught* playing catch with his sister's birthday cake—just minutes before her birthday party began.
- *caught* trying to glue the television set back together after having dropped it out a window.

Needless to say, Brewster was punished severely for every one of these crimes.

This was before he developed The Brewster Big Trouble Funniness Kit.

Now when Brewster is in big trouble (which is nearly always), he pulls out his kit; and before long, his parents, or his teacher, or the principal, or the neighbors, or even perfect strangers are holding their sides with laughter and forgetting just how eager they were to see Brewster thrashed within an inch of his life.

You will probably want to put together a kit just like Brewster's. Here's what it contains:

The Brewster Big Trouble Funniness Kit

3 oranges
1 very realistic squirrel mask
2 8-oz. water glasses attached to a long string
1 list of double-talk phrases
1 tube of flexible Day-Glo plastic
1 pair of track shoes

How does Brewster use the items in his kit? Well, we don't have to search very far to find an example.

Just last week, Brewster was chasing his dog through the living room. He tripped and cracked a mirror, ripped the new upholstery off the couch, pulled down the drapes, knocked the top off the piano, and tipped over the goldfish bowl. Standing ankle deep in water, he heard his mother approaching. Luckily, Brewster had The Brewster Big Trouble Funniness Kit with him.

"What's going on in here?" his mother cried, bursting angrily into the room.

Brewster pulled out the three oranges and began juggling them high over his head. His juggling caught his mother by surprise and kept her from noticing the water that was rapidly soaking into the carpet.

When she began to realize that something was amiss in the room, Brewster slipped on the squirrel mask and pretended to rummage for nuts. This usually got a huge laugh from his mother, who especially liked the way Brewster scratched his little squirrel whiskers, bunching up his fingers into little paws while continuing to keep the three oranges rotating in the air. This time, however, the squirrel mask did not amuse her.

So Brewster dropped the mask and the oranges and reached for the two 8-ounce water glasses. He tied them around his head with the string he had attached and said to his mother, "You wouldn't hit someone who wears glasses, would you?"

In the past, this had been his biggest laugh-getter. It had even gotten him off the hook the time he'd been caught dribbling his baby sister. But this time his mother just stood there, staring angrily at the soaked living room drapes that Brewster was still standing on.

Brewster quickly pulled out his list of double-talk phrases and began making funny excuses. "You see, Mom, I can explain everything. I was draling in the gream when the crale ronked my squeam. Heh heh heh."

A big laugh?

No—nothing.

Brewster was rapidly reaching the bottom of the kit. He dropped the double-talk phrase list and quickly pulled out the tube of soft Day-Glo plastic. He molded the plastic into the shape of a halo which he placed on top of his head. The glowing halo always got a laugh and always helped to remind her that he was still "Mommy's little angel."

But to Brewster's dismay, the halo was not working its usual heavenly magic. He watched his mother's face grow red with anger.

Quickly Brewster pulled out the final item from his kit, the item that never failed him—his track shoes. He slipped them on and ran out of the house as fast as he could.

Which brings us to the most important lesson of this chapter: A moving target is hardest to hit.

When You're in Big Trouble:
Excuses To Avoid if at All Possible

1. "I really don't know *how* the water got into the balloon."
2. "I know I'm late. I took a shortcut."
3. "It wasn't my fault that I failed the test. I copied off the wrong person!"
4. "I only wanted to scare him!"
5. "He ran into the snowball. I didn't throw it at him."
6. "How was I to know that five candy bars don't make a well-balanced lunch? They were different kinds."
7. "I only wanted to scare her!"
8. "I was just trying to show Billy what *not* to do so he'll know in the future that it is wrong."
9. "I can't be held responsible. All my actions are controlled by a brain-wave machine on a distant planet."
10. "I only wanted to scare it!"
11. "I didn't mean to take her doll, tear its head off, and paint its skin blue. It was an accident!"
12. "You should have *told* me not to accept dares."

QUESTIONS FOR REVIEW

1. What are the three funniest replies for when your mother says, "What do you think your punishment should be?"
2. When you are caught cheating on a test, is it funnier to fall off your chair and crawl out of the room or to bounce up onto your desk and leap out the window?
3. List the six funniest items to pad your jeans with just before getting a spanking.
4. True or false—You should always carry a big red hand with you to pull out when people say they've caught you red-handed.

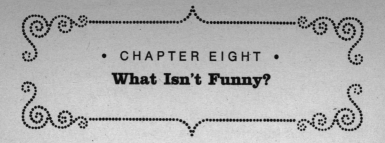

CHAPTER EIGHT

What Isn't Funny?

Well, here we are almost at the very end of this book. What a good place to put the final chapter!

So far we have talked about what *is* funny. Now, we're going to take a look at what *isn't* funny. So—no laughing this chapter!

Let's begin with the results of a recent survey. In this survey, more than 20,000 kids (most of them either your age or older or younger) were asked the question "What isn't funny?"

Nearly 15 of the kids came up with answers. On the following page are the results, the 12 least funny things in the world:

Unfunny thing	Percent of kids finding it unfunny
1. Cold chicken noodle soup	98
2. Everyone stomping on your new shoes	95
3. Getting punished for something you didn't do	83
4. Getting punished for something you did do	83
5. Getting more cold chicken noodle soup	75
6. Playing a game with someone who cheats	70
7. Playing a game with someone who won't cheat	68
8. Having to pose for family photographs	65
9. Having to kiss an aunt you don't like	60
10. Being the new kid in school	54
11. Being the new kid in school and getting cold chicken noodle soup	50
12. Being forced to answer questions in a silly survey	40

This survey offered a good start at finding out just what isn't funny. But the researchers were not satisfied. They decided to interview several kids and get longer answers from them. Again, the question was "What isn't funny?" Here are some of the things kids had to say:

"A few days ago, I dropped my hat on the playground. Some kids picked it up and started throwing it around. I asked them to give it back, but they wouldn't. I tried to grab it, but they kept throwing it back and forth out of my reach, and yelling, 'Keep away! Keep away!'

"They wouldn't give it back even when I started to cry. I think that playing keep-away is not funny—especially when it's *your* hat. I don't mind it so much if I'm throwing someone else's hat around."

"Sometimes I go to big parties where a lot of kids are invited—you know, birthday parties, surprise parties. A lot of us girls like to dance at these parties. But the boys won't dance. They spend all their time throwing the dinner rolls at each other.

"Last week I was at a party, and a boy came up to me. I thought he wanted to dance, but he just wanted to put an ice cube down my back. Now what's so funny about that?

"When I come home from a party, my back is always frozen and my party dress is soaking wet. It's not funny! Stop laughing."

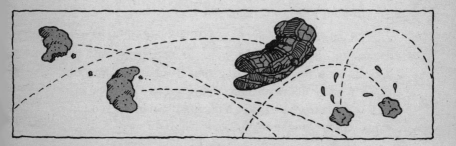

BRIAN QUIBBLE, *Fork in the Bend, Ohio*

"I'd just like to add that I never did get my hat back. They kept it, and I had to walk all the way home without a hat. I hope my mother doesn't notice."

FOSTER BADHABITS, *Bright Idea, Florida*

"Kids who laugh at other kids in math class are not funny. Let's face it, some kids just have a hard time with arithmetic. It's nothing to laugh at. If I can't work a problem at the chalkboard, it's because I just don't understand what I'm doing. You don't have to laugh at me, do you?

"And my dog *really did* chew up my math homework! Everyone thought that was funny, too. Well, it wasn't. Math class is not funny, and I don't think kids should be allowed to laugh in it."

NICK PICKER, *Long Island, Iowa*

"I'll tell you what isn't funny. When some aunt or uncle comes to visit, or maybe your grandparents, and you haven't seen them for a long time. And right away they start in with 'Oh, look how you've grown! Oh, you're so big! Oh, you're getting to be a big man!' And then you blush and everyone laughs at you.

"That isn't funny. Why do they always have to talk
about how big you've grown? All kids grow. It's no big
deal. I don't talk about how fat they are, or how old they
look, or how bald they're getting. *That* would be funny, but
I don't do it.

"I'm trying to stay as short as I can. Then they'll have
to say, 'Oh, look how short he's getting!' That'll confuse
them, and then I won't be embarrassed."

BRIAN QUIBBLE, *Fork in the Bend, Ohio*

"My mother found out about the hat. She just called
the other boys' mothers and told them about it. I'll tell you
what isn't funny. When your mother has to call someone
else's mother and ask for your hat back. That isn't funny
at all."

MARTHA WASHINGTON (*no relation*),
Silver Bullet, Maryland

"If you tell someone a secret, and she tells it to someone
else, and she tells it to someone else, and she tells it to
someone else, and she tells it to someone else, and she tells
it to someone else, and she tells it to someone else, and she
tells it to someone else, and she tells it to someone else,
and she tells it to someone else, and she tells it back to you
—that isn't funny. It sounds funny, but it isn't."

67

BENJIE BENN, Benjamin, Arkansas

"Pushing in the halls is not funny. A person could get hurt that way. Please don't use my name."

HECTOR WHIPPLE, Zig, Zag, North Dakota

"People call me Four Eyes. And I don't even wear glasses. I don't think that's very funny, do you?"

BENJIE BENN, Benjamin, Arkansas

"Using my name when I asked you not to isn't funny! Please don't do it a second time."

Most of the other answers were so unfunny they had us in tears. Does anyone have a clean handkerchief?

Jokes To Avoid at Any Cost!

1. Any joke that results in more than $20,000 in property damage.

2. Any joke that makes three or more people cry hysterically for hours afterwards.

3. Any joke that spoils someone's birthday.

4. Any joke that causes 4,000 people to run out of a crowded auditorium in terror.

5. Any joke that makes any member of your family wish that you were a member of any other family.

6. Any joke that hurts people's feelings so much they don't talk to you for the next 20 years.

7. Any joke that causes someone to blush in front of five or more people.

8. Any joke that ends in a world war.

9. Any joke that makes a sick person lose the desire to recover.

10. Any joke that involves tying an object that weighs more than 200 pounds to a dog's tail.

11. Any joke that makes a person feel no more than 4 and no less than 2 inches tall.

12. Any joke that brings down a plague of pestilence and boils on an entire city.

Bibliography

Many other books have been written on the subject of how to be funny. For some unfortunate reason, however, most of these books were printed on sponge cake rather than paper, and they fall apart when you turn the pages. Nevertheless, here are some other books on this subject you may wish to avoid.

Tom Foolery, *First Book of Funniness*, Chuckles Press, 1954.

Foolery has attempted to write a good beginner's book, but I'm afraid that his many chapters on how to be funny in the crib are just too babyish for most readers. Also, his chapter entitled "Being Funny with Three Oranges and a Grapefruit" is a complete waste of good fruit.

Tom Foolery, *First Book of Funny Faces*, Chuckles Press, 1955.

I'm sorry to say that this beginner's guide to making funny faces is also a failure. The instructions are hard to follow. And there are no pictures to show what the funny faces should look like. Also, the entire book is printed upside down for some mysterious reason.

O. B. Sirius, *How To Be Serious,* Pokerface Press, 1967.
Best book of its type. Excellent chapters on how not to tell jokes, how to miss the point of other people's jokes, and how not to be funny while wearing a false nose and glasses. Author has previously written *How To Be Nervous* and *How To Be Mistaken for Someone Else,* strange books that no one ever read.

Mark Thyme, *How To Be Funny with Apricots,* Duck Press, 1975.
A good idea that just doesn't work—mainly because apricots are not at all funny and never will be. Author has a few good suggestions for funny things to do with apricot pits, but once you've got them up your nose, what do you do for an encore?

Mark Thyme, *How To Be Funny with Melon Balls,* Duck Press, 1976.
One of the funniest and most helpful books on this subject ever written. Don't miss the chapter on how to slip melon balls secretly into someone's pockets. It will change your life.

Bonnie Lassie, *The Overhand Method of Throwing Pies,* Pants Press, 1976.
This is the book that started the whole controversy between those who throw pies overhanded and those who favor the underhand or sidearm approach. The book won several awards for Ms. Lassie—but it also got her plastered

with whipped cream and lemon meringue from angry partisans.

Bonnie Lassie, *Pie Throwing in Shakespeare's England,* Pants Press, 1976.

I just can't figure out why it took Ms. Lassie 650 pages to tell us that there was no pie throwing in Shakespeare's England. Neither could hundreds of angry playgoers, who showered her with pies of many varieties.

Bargil Krilgo, *Larf Larf Hoo Hoo,* Yellow Press, 1948.

This book does not seem to be written in any language known to humans. Perhaps it is all just a big put-on. It contains such chapters as "Scree Scree Wombo" and "Locum Lacum Boo." A complete waste of time, very confusing, and not a bit funny. Certainly not worth the $22.95 I paid for it.

Jerry Germ, *I Am the Funniest Person I Know,* Don't Press, 1970.

Warm and touching autobiography of the man who invented the dribble glass, itching powder, and the joy buzzer, because he "wanted to serve mankind and watch people shriek and cringe." When you open the cover of this splendid book, ink squirts out all over your clothes. A remarkable achievement. Unforgettable.

Jovial Rob Shine, *How To Be Funny,* Anonymous Press, 1776.

An out-and-out steal of this book. The author has copied this book word for word and has even copied my name. This is an outrage that must be dealt with in a court of law. Does anyone know a good lawyer?